Playmakers

Linebackers

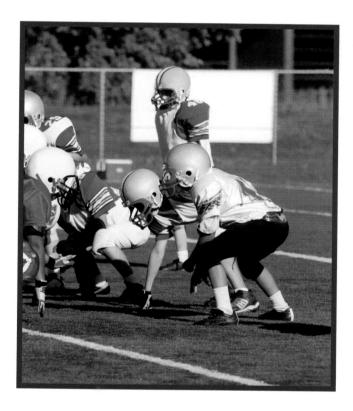

Tom Greve

ROURKE PUBLISHING
Vero Beach, Florida 32964

www.rourkepublishing.com

PHOTO CREDITS: © Tony Tremblay: Title Page, 5; © Jane Norton: 6; © Associated Press: 7, 12, 13, 16, 17, 18; © brian wilke: 9; © Suzanne Tucker: 11, 14; © james boulette: 15, 21; © Daniel Padavona: 19; © Strickke: 20; © Natalya Gerasimova: 22

Editor: Jeanne Sturm

Cover and page design by Tara Raymo

Library of Congress Cataloging-in-Publication Data

Greve, Tom.
 Linebackers / Tom Greve.
    p. cm. -- (Playmakers)
 Includes index.
 ISBN 978-1-60694-327-4 (hard cover)
 ISBN 978-1-60694-826-2 (soft cover)
 1. Linebackers (Football)--United States--Juvenile literature. I. Title.
 GV951.18.G73 2010
 796.332'24--dc22

                                                    2009006102

Printed in the USA

CG/CG

ROURKE PUBLISHING

www.rourkepublishing.com - rourke@rourkepublishing.com
Post Office Box 643328 Vero Beach, Florida 32964

Table of Contents

Linebackers

Tough, fast, and strong, linebackers form the heart and soul of a football team's defense.

They play in front of the **defensive backs** and behind the **defensive line,** which is why the position is called linebacker. They make plays by stopping the other team from advancing the ball toward the end zone.

Playmaker's FACT WITH IMPACT

Linebackers' teammates on the defensive line engage the other team's offensive linemen along the **line of scrimmage.** This allows the linebackers to swarm toward the ball carrier without getting blocked.

Linebackers first identify which player on offense has the ball, and then tackle that player as quickly as possible.

Linebackers usually have the greatest combination of size, strength, and speed of all the defensive players. Size and strength helps them fight off blockers and tackle ball carriers who break through the line. Speed helps them pursue, catch, and tackle the other team's ball carriers.

It takes strength, balance, and vision to fight through several blockers and tackle the ball carrier.

The Chicago Bears player Brian Urlacher is one of the best current pro linebackers.

Brian Urlacher stands 6 feet 4 inches (1.9 meters) tall and weighs 260 pounds (118 kilograms). Despite his massive size, he can run 40 yards (37 meters) in less than 5 seconds. He won the Defensive Rookie of the Year award in 2000 and was the NFL's Defensive Player of the Year in 2005.

Skills on the Inside

There are two types of linebackers. There are inside linebackers (ILBs) and outside linebackers (OLBs).

Most defensive **formations** use one inside linebacker and two outside linebackers. The inside linebacker is called the middle linebacker. Some defenses use two inside and two outside linebackers.

Playmaker's FACT WITH IMPACT

Typically, defenses use four defensive linemen with three linebackers behind them. This is a 4-3 defensive formation. Sometimes, teams will use three linemen and four linebackers; this is called the 3-4 defense.

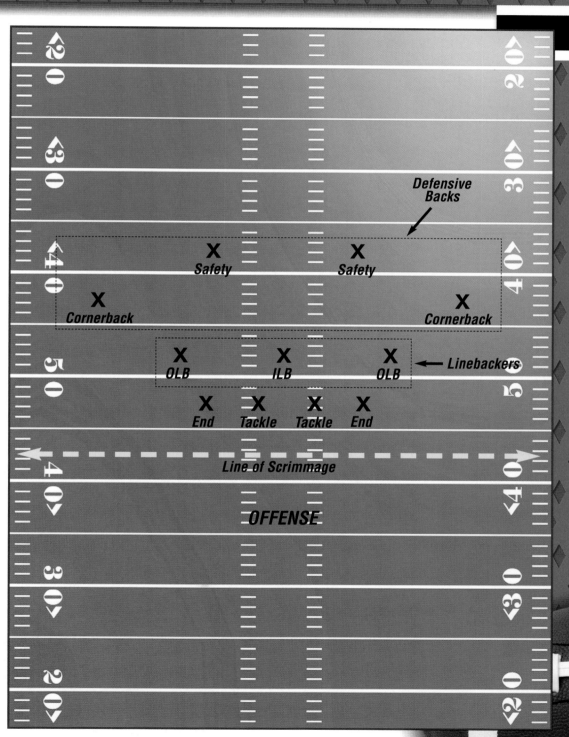

A Typical 4-3 Defensive Line-Up

The middle linebacker is the **quarterback** of the defense. He covers the field from sideline to sideline tackling the opponent's ball carrier while avoiding blockers. When the opponent's quarterback passes, middle linebackers react into pass-coverage position.

These responsibilities require quick movement forward, backward, and side-to-side.

The middle linebacker is usually responsible for relaying the coach's instructions and directing the defense on the field.

Hall-of-Famer Dick Butkus played for the Chicago Bears. He is a classic example of a middle linebacker.

Dick Butkus was a tough, competitive, standout athlete. Born and raised in Chicago, he played middle linebacker for his hometown Bears from 1965 through 1973. His intense hard-hitting style caused opponents to avoid his part of the field. Many players to come after Butkus's time have tried to copy his no-nonsense demeanor on the field.

Skills on the Outside

Outside linebackers also have to be able to run down ball carriers and tackle them while avoiding blockers. They **patrol** one side or corner of the defense. Like the middle linebacker, outside linebackers have to be able to instantly identify passing situations and react immediately.

Playing outside linebacker requires short bursts of speed and the ability to change direction to get into position to defend against passes.

The quarterback sack is among the most exciting plays a linebacker can make.

When the offense runs the ball toward the sides of the field, outside linebackers must try to tackle the ball carrier, or at least force the ball carrier back toward the rest of the pursuing defense so someone else can make the tackle.

On college or pro teams, outside linebackers are required to pressure the passer on obvious passing downs. Sometimes outside linebackers will lead their team in quarterback **sacks**.

Lawrence Taylor was such a good outside linebacker, he changed the way the position was played during his career with the New York Giants.

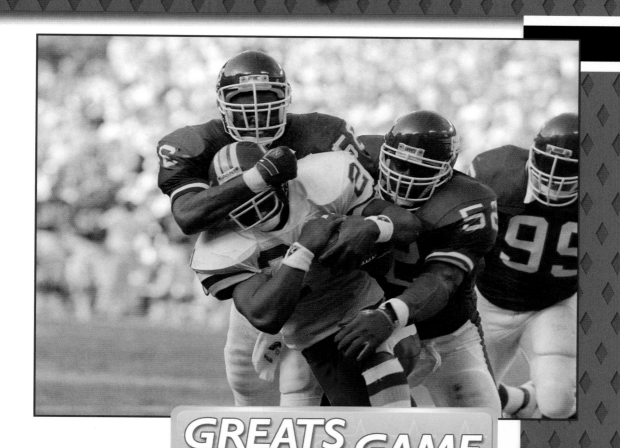

GREATS of the GAME

Lawrence Taylor was the greatest pass-rushing linebacker in the history of pro football. He was so good at pressuring the quarterback that nowadays, defenses expect one or both of their outside linebackers to go after the quarterback when he drops back to pass. Opposing teams often used two or more players to try to keep Taylor away from their quarterback. He played from 1980 until 1993. He was enshrined in the Pro Football Hall of Fame in 1999.

So You Want to Be a Linebacker?

Prepare for impact! Linebackers usually make the most tackles of all the players on a defense. That means they are willing and able to create collisions with other players and bring down the opponent's ball carrier on nearly every play. They spend hours in practice performing **drills** to learn proper tackling techniques.

Learning proper tackling technique helps linebackers avoid injuries.

Linebackers love to make big hits on the ball carrier.
These hits energize fans and teammates.

Linebackers play defense, but they can still score touchdowns by picking up a **fumble** or by **intercepting** a pass and running it back for a score. For linebackers, fumble recoveries and interceptions, like quarterback sacks, are the biggest plays they can make.

When linebackers intercept a pass, it can change the outlook or momentum of the game.

Linebackers work together as a single unit stopping the opponent from advancing the ball. Sometimes, they all come together to make a gang tackle.

Playing the position of linebacker is like a demolition dance. It involves making quick, smooth movements toward the ball, rolling off or casting aside blockers along the way, and then colliding with the ball carrier to tackle him.

If this kind of rough-and-tumble action sounds like fun, then you might be ready to put on the pads and start learning how to play linebacker.

Glossary

defensive backs (di-FEN-siv BAKS): safeties and cornerbacks, the last line of a football team's defense

defensive line (di-FEN-siv LINE): tackles and ends, the front of a football team's defense

drills (DRILZ): repetitive actions meant to teach a skill

formations (for-MAY-shuhnz): the placement of players at the start of a play

fumble (FUHM-buhl): when the ball is knocked loose from a ball carrier

intercepting (in-tuhr-SEPT-ing): when a defensive player catches a pass thrown by the other team's quarterback

line of scrimmage (LINE ov SKRIM-ij): an imaginary border stretching from the ball to each sideline along which both the offensive and defensive lines get into position at the start of a play

patrol (puh-TROL): to watch over, or be on guard against something

quarterback (KWOR-tur-bak): field general

sacks (SAKS): tackles of the other team's quarterback made behind the line of scrimmage

Index

Websites to Visit

www.dickbutkus.com/Biography.aspx
www.kidzworld.com/article/5039-quiz-the-coach-how-to-play-linebacker
football.about.com/cs/football101/a/positiondef.htm

About the Author

Tom Greve lives in Chicago with his wife, Meg, and
their two children, Madison and William. He enjoys
playing, watching, and writing about sports.